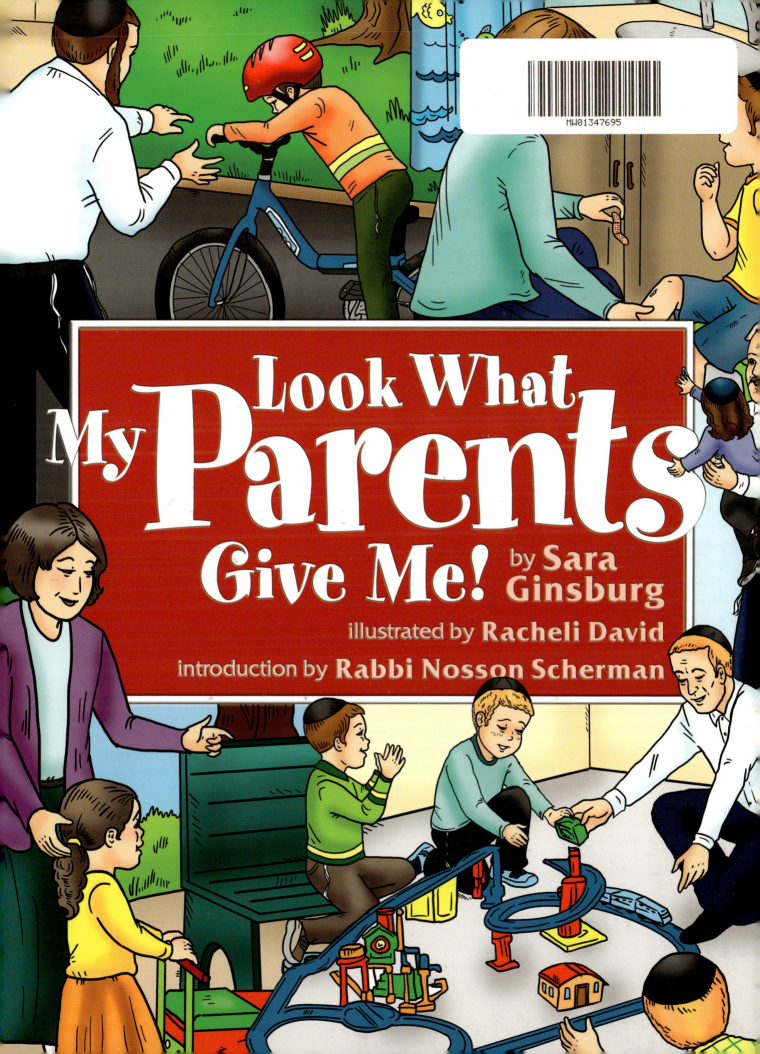

> *Dedicated in memory of*
> **my beloved parents** עליהם השלום,
> *Who gave me all this and much more.*
>
> יהי זכרם ברוך

ARTSCROLL® YOUTH SERIES

"LOOK WHAT MY PARENTS GIVE ME"

© Copyright 2014 by Mesorah Publications, Ltd.
First edition – First impression: April 2014

ALL RIGHTS RESERVED

No part of this book may be reproduced **in any form,** photocopy, electronic media, or otherwise – even FOR PERSONAL, STUDY GROUP, OR CLASSROOM USE – without **written** permission from the copyright holder, except by a reviewer who wishes to quote brief passages in connection with a review written for inclusion in magazines or newspapers.

THE RIGHTS OF THE COPYRIGHT HOLDER WILL BE STRICTLY ENFORCED.

Published by **MESORAH PUBLICATIONS, LTD.**
4401 Second Avenue / Brooklyn, N.Y 11232 / (718) 921-9000 / Fax: (718) 680-1875
www.artscroll.com

Illustrated by Racheli David, david039328958@gmail.com

Distributed in Israel by **SIFRIATI / A. GITLER**
Moshav Magshimim / Israel

Distributed in Europe by **LEHMANNS**
Unit E, Viking Business Park, Rolling Mill Road / Jarrow, Tyne and Wear / England NE32 3DP

Distributed in Australia and New Zealand by **GOLDS WORLD OF JUDAICA**
3-13 William Street / Balaclava, Melbourne 3183, Victoria, Australia

Distributed in South Africa by **KOLLEL BOOKSHOP**
Northfield Centre / 17 Northfield Avenue / Glenhazel 2192 / Johannesburg, South Africa

Printed in the United States of America by Noble Book Press Corp.
Custom bound by Sefercraft, Inc. / 4401 Second Avenue / Brooklyn N.Y, 11232

ISBN-10: 1-4226-1489-1
ISBN-13: 978-1-4226-1489-1

Introduction

BY RABBI NOSSON SCHERMAN

Our Chachamim tell us that there are three partners in every person: Hashem, his father, and his mother. When partners own something, each of them wants it to succeed, and each partner tries his best to make sure it has everything it needs.

Hashem gives us eyes to see, ears to hear, a mind to think, and all the other things we need to have a good life. He gives us sunshine, the food we eat, the water we drink, and all the other things we need to grow and have a good life.

Hashem gives us so much that it is impossible to thank Him enough. Did you ever think that we could say the same thing about our mothers and fathers? Did you ever think about all the wonderful things they do for us?

In this wonderful book, with its beautiful rhymes and pictures, we'll see how every day is filled with things our parents do all the time. Even though we **know** about these things, we don't always **think** about them. But we **should** think about them. So let's start turning the pages and listening to the rhymes and looking at the pictures.

As we read, we will understand two mitzvos of the Torah. Hashem wants us to **honor** our parents – that means to do things that show them how much we love them. And Hashem wants us to **respect** them – that means to treat them as if they were a king who could punish us if we do something wrong. After all, they are Hashem's partners, and He wants us to be good to His partners.

You will enjoy this book. And when you read it, you'll think about everything your parents do for you – and you'll love them even more.

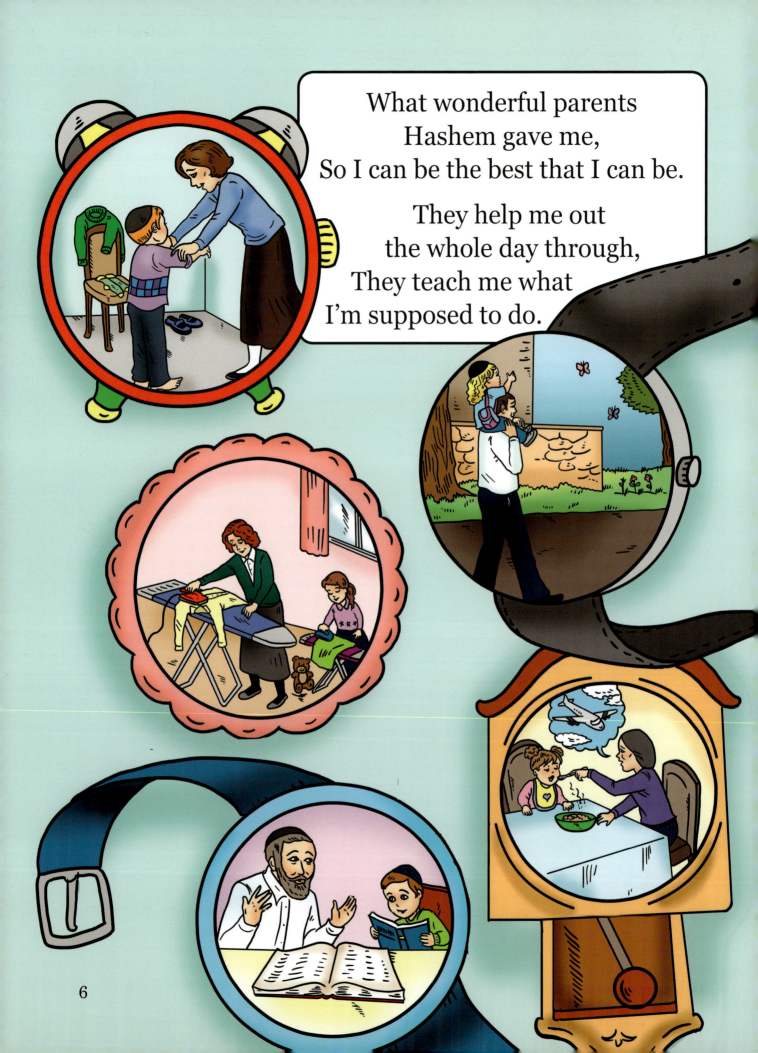

To watch Mommy light the candles bright,
To listen to Kiddush on Friday night.

To hug me tightly when I feel sad,
To show how much they love me so I'll feel glad.

When I grow up you'll be proud of me,
I'll be the best that I can be.
For I have partners like no other,
Hashem, my father, and my mother!